Tower of Babel

To Luis, Mateo and the new lodger, for so many yellow buttons. —C.R.

KAR-BEN PUBLISHING
A division of Lerner Publishing Group, Inc.
241 First Avenue North
Minneapolis, MN 55401 U.S.A.
1-800-4-Karben

Website address: www.karben.com

Library of Congress Cataloging-in-Publication Data

Gadot, A. S., 1944–
    Tower of Babel / by Arnona Sever Gadot ; illustrated by Cecilia Rebora.
        p.   cm.
    Summary: Based on a Biblical story, the people of Shinar build a tower so high that no one can understand what anyone else is saying, and the formerly friendly citizens stop communicating with one another.
        ISBN 978–0–8225–9917–3 (lib. bdg. : alk. paper)
        [1. Babel, Tower of—Fiction.] I. Rebora, Cecilia, ill. II. Title.
    PZ7.G11716To 2010
    [E]—dc22   2008033483

Manufactured in the United States of America
1 – VI – 12/15/09

Tower of Babel

by A.S. GADOT

illustrated by CECILIA REBORA

Years ago
many, many years ago

All the people in the world lived
in one small valley in the Land of Shinar.

They spoke one language,
and this was very convenient.

They had no problem whatsoever
understanding each other.

Every morning the sun rose on the valley,
and every evening the sun sank.

Between sunrise and sunset, the people
did exactly the same things.

They went to school,

worked at their jobs,

and kept their homes tidy
and gardens blooming.

In the evenings they gathered
at the café to relax with a cup of tea.

The waitress would ask, "With lemon? With sugar?
And how about a piece of cheesecake?"

Or say, "The strudel is excellent today."
And everyone would understand her.

Then they would discuss important issues, such as
"What's the difference between 'always' and 'forever'?"

Or, "Why doesn't Purim come twice a year?"

Or, "Is a pocket with a hole
in it— and nothing else—empty or full?"

Later, they slept peacefully and dreamed of nothing in particular.

The days in the valley passed,

Day, after day,
after day.

Nothing ever happened, neither good nor bad.

And that was very boring.

Until one evening at the café,
someone jumped to his feet and shouted:

"I wish something would
happen in the Valley of Shinar!"

"Yes," called his friend from the
other side of the room.

"Something that never happened
before," the waitress added.

"Something that will never happen
again!" the cook proposed.

"My sentiments exactly!" said the old professor, stroking his parrot who squawked in agreement.

It was absolutely clear. The time had come for something new, something unusual, to happen in the Valley of Shinar.

But what?

Someone suggested starting a band and
going on a tour around the world.

But at that time there was no one else in
the world, so the suggestion fell flat.

Another proposed forming a government and making important decisions.

But nobody could figure out what they would decide.

Someone else suggested searching the Internet,

But the computer hadn't been invented yet.

In the end, a little boy shouted
from the kitchen window.
"Let's build a tower!
Let's build a tower that will reach heaven!
A tower that will make us important and powerful!"
And to this they all agreed.

Heaven was such an interesting place—
With twinkling stars,
And a moon that grew bigger and smaller,
And clouds that changed form and floated away.

None of them had ever been to heaven!

They didn't waste time on plans,
but started right away...
Some digging the foundation,
Some dragging wood,
Some cutting stones,
Some raising scaffolds,
And some counting the floors.

They worked together happily,
and the tower started towering.

They built the first floor and the second,
the third and the fourth.

When they got to the 20th floor, they
organized a picnic between the pillars.

Everybody came.

When they reached the 50th floor, they held a dance.

The conga line went on into the wee hours of the night.

When they reached the 100th floor, they congratulated themselves.

"How close we are to heaven," they agreed.

"We will rule the earth and the sky!"

Suddenly, lightning tore through the sky.
Thunder crashed, and a heavy rain began to fall.
There was hail the size of golf balls.
The people of the valley hid under
the scaffolds, scared and shivering.

Then the rain stopped.

The sun smiled between the clouds.

The people of the Valley of Shinar looked
at each other and started to speak.

But no one could understand
a word that was said.

The architects
spoke Dutch

And the engineers,
Chinese.

The stone-cutters spoke French,

The woodworkers, Japanese.

The painters spoke Italian,
The carpenters, Portuguese.

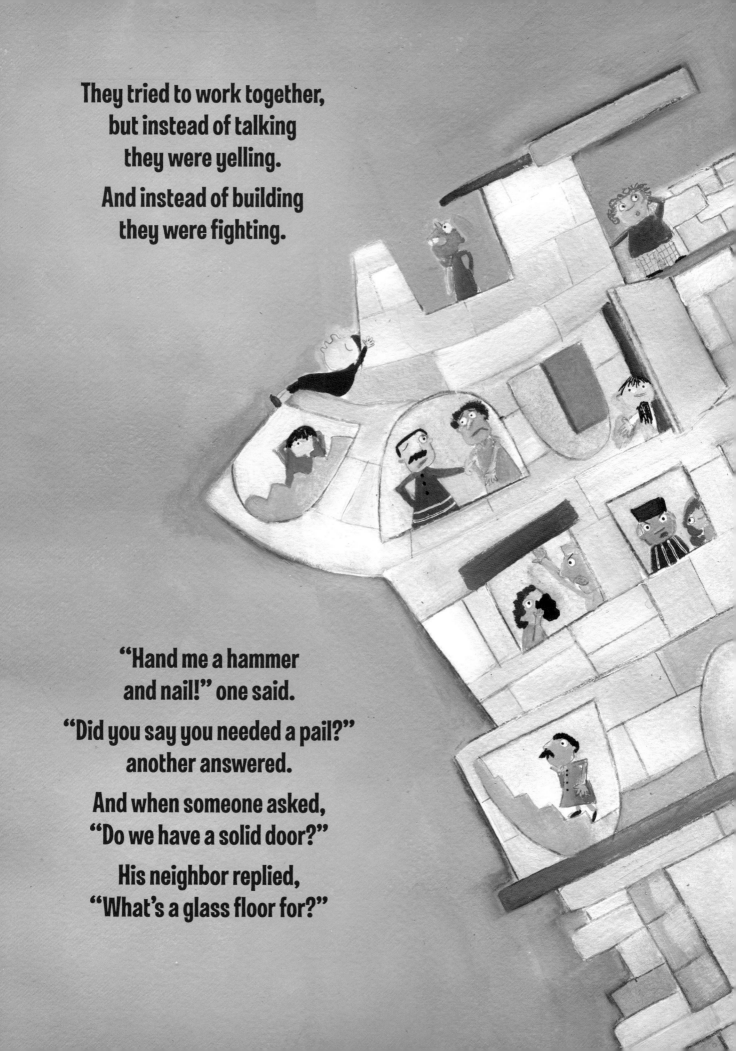

They tried to work together,
but instead of talking
they were yelling.

And instead of building
they were fighting.

"Hand me a hammer
and nail!" one said.

"Did you say you needed a pail?"
another answered.

And when someone asked,
"Do we have a solid door?"

His neighbor replied,
"What's a glass floor for?"

Soon they were all squabbling.

The tower that once looked straight and strong started to look lopsided and shaky.

The staircases were so crooked that people climbed round and round to nowhere.

Once tall and proud, the tower was now a giant pretzel.

This could not go on.

So the building of the tower stopped.

And the people of the valley packed their belongings and prepared to leave.

The Italians built gondolas and sailed for Venice.

The Chinese rode their bicycles to Beijing.

The Dutch danced toward Amsterdam on their big wooden clogs.

One after another they departed.

And soon there was no one left
in the Valley of Shinar—
except for the old professor,
who camped out on a
crooked balcony with his parrot.

And, from time to time, he
picked up a brick and laid it
in one direction or another.

Years later, many, many years later,
**the tower became known
as the Tower of Babel,**

Because the building was stopped when
people couldn't talk to each other.

They could only babble.